Raising the princess to love herself

Raising the princess to love herself

IT WAS EARLY MORNING IN THE SUMMERTIME, SHE OPENED HER EYES AND WATCHED THE SUNSHINE. TWINKLE IN HER EYE, LIKE PRETTY BUTTERFLIES. HAIR SO NATURAL KINKY AND FINE.

she brushed her teeth
and ate her some breakfast.
Seeds in her fruit and her foods organic..

She played outside and not
on her tablet.
a little princess with a big intuition.

PRETTY BROWN SKIN AND
HER MOTHER Was CHOCOLATE.
BLACK GIRl MAGIC,
SHE CAME FROM A GODDESS!!

SHE KNEW WITHOUT BRAINS
HER BEAUTY WAS NOTHING.HER
DAD TAUGHT HER THAT &
HE GAVE HER PROTECTION....

SHE GREW UP TO BE A
STRONG BLACK WOMAN!

THE END

YOUR BEAUTIFUL
LITTLE PRINCESS

YOUR INTELLIGENT LITTLE PRINCESS

THE WORLD NEEDS YOU LITTLE PRINCESS